Going Up!

A COLOR COUNTING BOOK BY
PETER SIS

GREENWILLOW BOOKS  NEW YORK

Going Up!

For my grandmother,
who doesn't have an elevator

Pen-and-ink and watercolor paints were used for
the full-color art. The text type is Kabel Book.

Library of Congress Cataloging-in-Publication Data
Sis, Peter.
Going up! by / Peter Sis.
p.   cm.
Summary: As the elevator moves up from
the first floor to the twelfth, various people
dressed in different colors get on, all bound
for a birthday surprise.
ISBN 0-688-08125-8.
ISBN 0-688-08127-6 (lib. bdg.)
[1. Elevators—Fiction.   2. Color—Fiction.
3. Apartment houses—Fiction.
4. Birthdays—Fiction.
5. Counting.]   I. Title.
PZ7.S6219Go 1989   [E]—dc19
87-37203   CIP   AC

Mary bought the flowers.

Everyone in the building was getting ready.

Mary got in the elevator on the 1st floor.

A witch with a black violin case got in on the 2nd floor.

A chef in a white hat got in on the 3rd floor.

Little Red Riding Hood got in on the 4th floor.

A yellow banana got in on the 5th floor.

An astronaut in a blue space suit got in on the 6th floor.

A surgeon in green got in on the 7th floor.

A clown in an orange costume got in on the 8th floor.

A brown bear got in on the 9th floor.

A girl in a gray wetsuit got in on the 10th floor.

A king in a purple robe got in on the 11th floor.

They all got off on the 12th floor—

and shouted SURPRISE! SURPRISE!

and HAPPY BIRTHDAY! to Mary's mother.

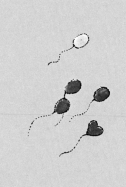